Jayylen's Juneteenth Surprise

A Little Golden Book®

By Lavaille Lavette
Illustrated by David Wilkerson

Copyright © 2023 by Lavette Books, Inc.
All rights reserved. Published in the United States by Golden Books, an imprint of Random House Children's Books, a division of Penguin Random House LLC, 1745 Broadway, New York, NY 10019, by arrangement with Lavette Books, Inc. Golden Books, A Golden Book, A Little Golden Book, the G colophon, and the distinctive gold spine are registered trademarks of Penguin Random House LLC. Jayylen™ is a trademark of Lavette Books.
rhcbooks.com
lavettebooks.com
Educators and librarians, for a variety of teaching tools, visit us at RHTeachersLibrarians.com
Library of Congress Control Number: 2022947567
ISBN 978-0-593-56814-9 (trade) — ISBN 978-0-593-56815-6 (ebook)
Printed in the United States of America
10 9 8 7 6 5 4 3 2 1

"**No way!**" Jayylen's jaw dropped as he looked at the sign. Then, a big smile spread over his face.

He thought back to a morning a few weeks earlier. . . .

He had been fast asleep when Paw Paw Jimmy's shout woke him up.

"Aha! Found it!"

Jayylen sat up and watched Paw Paw Jimmy slip on the weirdest-looking vest he had ever seen.

"Now that is one fine frottoir," Paw Paw Jimmy said.

"Fro-twahr?" Jayylen asked, trying to get the word right. "What's it for?"

"For playin' zydeco, of course. Yes, sir! We gon' do a little two-steppin' dance at our Juneteenth celebration."

Jayylen shook his head. He knew Paw Paw Jimmy was speaking English, but nothing he was saying made any sense! What was zydeco? And what was Juneteenth?

Jayylen was still trying to figure out what Paw Paw Jimmy was talking about when he slid into his seat at the kitchen table.

"I declare!" Paw Paw Jimmy cried, sitting down next to Jayylen. "Now that you all have moved back home from the big city, I'll have some time to teach you more about our family traditions! Who doesn't know zydeco? And with Juneteenth comin' up."

"Now, Daddy," Jayylen's momma, Helen, said. "You know we haven't had a Juneteenth celebration around here in a long time!"

Paw Paw Jimmy waved his hand. "I know, I know. But that's all changing." He slapped his knee and rose to his feet. "This year, we celebrate!"

"Um, Momma," Jayylen began. "What's Juneteenth?"

"On Juneteenth, we remember June 19, 1865. That was the day when enslaved African Americans in Galveston, Texas, finally learned that they were free," Momma said. "Back then, it took almost two and a half years after the Emancipation Proclamation for the news to reach them. Every year on June nineteenth, people across America celebrate freedom and strength by remembering that day in 1865."

"What are 'enslaved' people?" Jayylen asked.
"Enslaved people are people who are forced to work without pay," Momma explained.
"Kind of like us when you force us to do chores!" Jayylen's big sister, Hazel, said, coming into the kitchen.

"Not at all like chores." Momma shook her head. "You see, back then, many African people were taken from their countries. A lot of them were brought to America, where they were forced to do hard work and treated very poorly."

"That's right," Paw Paw Jimmy said. "The terrible practice of enslaving African American people in America came to an end when President Abraham Lincoln issued the Emancipation Proclamation."

"So what's zydeco? And what does it have to do with Juneteenth?" Jayylen asked.

"Zydeco may not have been around for the first Juneteenth, but music's always been our folks' way of celebrating," Paw Paw Jimmy said with a smile. "And there's nothin' quite like zydeco to make you want to dance!"

Paw Paw Jimmy swiped through his phone. "Just listen. You'll see. This here is Beau Frank. He is one *fiiiine* zydeco singer—one of the best there is—and my favorite."

Paw Paw Jimmy stood up and put on his frottoir. He tapped his foot. He bobbed his head. Then, with his spoon, he played along on his frottoir. "There. You feel that? Magic in the air."

Jayylen did feel it. The music coursed through him and his feet started tapping to the beat.

"That's our music," Paw Paw Jimmy said. "And don't you forget it, Jayylen!"

"Paw Paw Jimmy, can you teach me to play the frottoir?" Jayylen asked.

So Paw Paw Jimmy taught Jayylen how to play the frottoir. He practiced every day. Jayylen loved playing along to the zydeco music almost as much as he loved making new inventions with his engineering kits.

Now Jayylen stared at the sign. Beau Frank was here . . . in his town. He was playing at Junita's Restaurant that afternoon! Jayylen knew just what to do.

He raced home and grabbed Paw Paw Jimmy's frottoir, then ran back out the door.

A big, strong woman looked down at Jayylen and frowned as he approached the restaurant. "Aren't you a little young to be here alone?" she asked.

Jayylen nodded. "Probably. It's just that tomorrow is Juneteenth. My Paw Paw Jimmy told me all about it. He's hosting a Juneteenth celebration, and he just loves Mr. Beau Frank, so I thought—"

"Sorry, kid." The woman smiled kindly. "I'd love to help you, but Mr. Frank is busy getting ready for his show."

Jayylen's heart sank. "I understand," he whispered.

As he turned to go, he felt Paw Paw Jimmy's frottoir on his chest. Grabbing a spoon from his bag, he made up a song similar to the one Paw Paw Jimmy had first played for him. Jayylen closed his eyes and two-stepped to his beat.

Before long, a large crowd surrounded him. They were dancing, clapping, and singing along. "Hey, you're pretty good!" a voice said.

Jayylen opened his eyes and found himself face to face with Beau Frank!

Jayylen's heart pounded. This was it—his chance! "My Paw Paw Jimmy loves you, and we're having a Juneteenth celebration, and I just wanted to know if you would consider coming—I mean, if you can get away, that is. It would be the best surprise ever for my Paw Paw Jimmy."

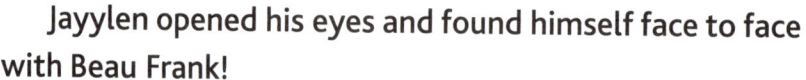

Beau Frank laughed. "I think I got all that," he said. "And I'll tell you what, I'd be happy to attend your Juneteenth celebration tomorrow—as long as you agree to play with me!"

The next day, Jayylen watched as Beau Frank made his way onto the stage. Beside him, Paw Paw Jimmy was so surprised he jumped for joy. "What . . . how . . . ?" he stuttered.

Jayylen grabbed Paw Paw Jimmy and hugged him tight. "Surprise! Happy Juneteenth, Paw Paw Jimmy!" he said. "Now, if you'll excuse me, I've got a show to play!"

And that's just what Jayylen did.